MEET ALL THESE FRIENDS IN BUZZ BOOKS:

Thomas the Tank Engine
The Animals of Farthing Wood
James Bond Junior
Fireman Sam
Blinky Bill
Joshua Jones
Rupert
Babar

First published in Great Britain in 1994
by Buzz Books
an imprint of Reed Children's Books
Michelin House, 81 Fulham Road, London SW3 6RB
and Auckland, Melbourne, Singapore and Toronto

ISBN 1 85591 368 2

Printed in Italy by Olivotto

ROCK 'N' RIDE

Story by Norman Redfern
Illustrations by Arkadia

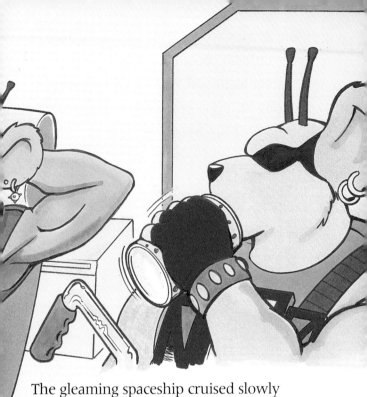

The gleaming spaceship cruised slowly
through space. To its crew – Throttle,
Vinnie and Modo – it seemed like just
another day. So they turned up the music,
put a motorcycle race on the video, and
grabbed a few ice-cold sodas!

"Now, this is living guys," said Modo.
"Nothin' to do but rockin' and rollin' and
racing through the cosmos. We've got
absolutely no problems!"

But as he spoke, a Plutarkian destroyer spotted their spaceship.

"Target identified, sir," said the Plutarkian lookout. "It's one of a type used only by the Cave Mice from Mars."

"Very well," said his Commander. "Gunner! Blow that ship to the seven scattered galaxies – now!"

The attack was swift. Plutarkian missiles rocked the spaceship. Throttle fought to control it, but it was no good.

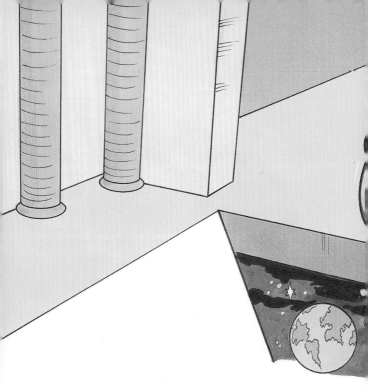

"What're we gonna do?" asked Modo.

"That's easy," replied Throttle. "We're going down!"

The ship was falling fast towards an unknown planet.

"Modo!" Throttle yelled. "Get 'em ready to eject!"

Modo set the controls and then rushed

to join Vinnie and Throttle. At the back of the
ship, a shutter opened, and there they were –
three gleaming, high-powered motorcycles.

"Helmets on!" ordered Throttle. "It's time to
rock. . . and ride!"

The Biker Mice kick-started their motorcycles and waited, engines roaring, until it
was time to eject.

On Planet Earth, in a city called Chicago, a baseball game was about to begin. Suddenly, a bright light burned in the dark sky above the stadium. The crowd gasped as a spaceship fell towards the ground.

Then, as it was about to crash, three
motorbikes roared out of the side of the
spaceship and landed in the middle of the
pitch. The crowd went wild.

"Didn't mean to cause any trouble, Citizens,"
said Throttle, saluting the crowd. "O.K., bro's –
kick it!"

Engines roaring, the Biker Mice showed the crowd one last wheelie, then raced for the exits. Vinnie steered his bike up a flight of stairs. He skidded round the corner, to find two people blocking his way. And one of them was armed!

14

Vinnie raced towards the kid with the crowbar. He grabbed the weapon, flipped it into the air and blasted it with his vape cannon. The crowbar disappeared.

"I'm out of here!" said the kid, running faster than he'd ever run before.

Vinnie turned to the older one.

"Thanks, Mister," said the hot dog man. "Here – have a dog!"

"Dog, eh? I'll check it out," said Vinnie. "Ride free, Citizen!"

He met Throttle and Modo in the stadium car park.

"Let's roll!" cried Throttle, speeding away down the deserted Chicago street. On either side of the road, tall buildings had been flattened, and huge holes dug in the ground.

17

Suddenly, Throttle skidded to a halt. Something was wrong with his bike.

"Busted gyro," he told his friends.

"Look at the bright side," said Vinnie, pointing across the street.

One building was still standing – the Last Chance Garage.

"I'll scope it out," said Vinnie.

Inside the garage was Chicago's best motor-cycle mechanic. Her name was Charley, and she had one big problem – a slippery customer called Greasepit.

His boss, Lawrence Limburger, had been buying up buildings and knocking them down. Now he wanted the Last Chance Garage.

"And what Lawrence Limburger wants," said Greasepit, "Lawrence Limburger gets."

20

Greasepit oozed grease. Wherever he went, he left an oily trail behind him. He moved towards Charley. Charley tried to dodge him, but she slipped on a patch of oil and landed on the floor.

Greasepit stood over her, holding Lawrence Limburger's contract.

"How about signing now, lady?" he growled.

"Say there, Citizen," came a voice from the doorway, "Why don't you leave the lady alone?"

"And who's gonna make me?" snarled Greasepit.

"'Who's-Gonna-Make-Me?' is my middle name," said Vinnie.

22

He grabbed a rope from the garage ceiling
and swung towards the oily bully. His fists
ready, Vinnie let go of the rope – and landed
in a pool of grease. He slid across the floor and
hit the wall.

"Get up and fight," taunted Greasepit. "What
are ya – a man or a mouse?"

With a crash, Modo and Throttle burst in
through the windows.

"A mouse," said Modo.

"Now…it's tail whippin' time!" said Throttle.

Modo curled his tail around Greasepit's
ankles. Throttle fired a ray at the tyre rack
above Greasepit's head. One by one, the tyres
fell around Greasepit's feet, legs and body.

Soon he was up to his neck in tyres. Modo tugged his tail away sharply, and Greasepit spun to the floor.

"Tell your boss The Biker Mice From Mars are in town," said Throttle.

"Time to roll, sweetheart," said Vinnie.

25

He kicked the tyres, and Greasepit rolled out
of the Last Chance Garage.

Throttle turned to Charley.

"You O.K., ma'am?" he asked.

"Don't you come any closer!" she cried.

"We just came in to get my bike fixed," said Throttle.

"Yeah," said Modo, "we're the good guys."

"But you're mice!" said Charley. "Where on Earth did you come from?"

"Mars," said Modo.

"It's a long story," said Throttle.

"And we're hungry," said Vinnie.

"Well, I know a great cheese shop," said Charley.

"Cheese? Yuck!" said the mice.

"How about a couple of hot dogs?" suggested Vinnie.

First, Charley had to repair Throttle's bike. After a quick tune-up, the engines were roaring again. But this time Vinnie had a passenger.

"Right," he said, "let's rock – "

And Throttle, Modo, and Charley all joined in – "and RIDE!"